THE BOYS' ROOM

TRANSGENDER EROTICA

SHAE'S T-GIRL ADVENTURES
BOOK 4

VICTORIA RUSH

VOLUME 4

SHAE'S T-GIRL ADVENTURES - BOOK 4

COPYRIGHT

The Boys's Room © 2024 Victoria Rush

Cover Design © 2024 PhotoMaras

For the uninhibited...

1

When our cabaret troupe finished its tour of the western states, I decided to rent a car and drive the long way back to Chicago to unwind and catch my breath. The drive through Montana and the Dakotas was breathtaking, with grassy ranch land and undulating wheat fields that stretched on for miles. It was nice to have some alone time to collect my thoughts and appreciate the natural beauty of the external landscape. I'd spent so much time performing in busy nightclubs and holed up in cramped hotels that I was beginning to go stir-crazy. But after a few hours on the road, I felt the need to pee, and I decided to stop at a roadside truck stop to empty my bladder.

The diner was busier than usual with long weekend travelers, and when I headed over to the ladies' restroom, there was a long lineup of patrons waiting to use the facilities. After tapping my foot nervously for ten minutes, I glanced over at the adjacent men's room, noticing a steady inflow and outflow of customers zipping up their pants. When I couldn't hold it any longer, I said *fuck it* and walked nonchalantly into the main portico, noticing a long line of empty urinals. Some of the men washing their hands next to the large mirror over the sinks looked up and squinted their eyes when they saw a woman enter the private lavatory, and when I headed over to one of the urinals, their eyes flared open as the water splashed over the front of their pants.

It must have been a strange sight seeing a woman unzipping her pants in front of a urinal, but in this enlightened age of fluid gender rights, it couldn't have been the first time they'd heard of cross-gender bathroom use, even in the redneck state of Montana. But as I pulled out my penis to empty my urine into the basin, suddenly two other men walked up beside me, noisily unzipping their pants and spraying their piss noisily into their basins. I could feel their eyes staring down at my shrinking package while I strained to start my flow, but as hard as I tried, nothing would come out.

Shit, I cursed under my breath. *Perfect time to have a shy bladder.*

"What's the matter, sweetheart?" the man on my left chuckled. "Cat got your tongue?"

"More like her *dick,*" the man on my opposite side mocked. "If you can call it that. That worm looks more like *fish bait* to me."

"Do you need us to nibble on it to help you wet yourself?" the first man sniggered.

"Or perhaps we could hold it for you while one of us massages your *prostate*? That usually helps a bit–"

"Fuck you, *assholes,*" I said, stepping back from the urinal and zipping up my pants. "Have you ever heard of bathroom etiquette? Or treating a lady with respect?"

"Possibly," the first man said, winking at his companion. "But you ain't no lady."

"Whatever," I said, strutting over to the last open cubicle next to the far wall and slamming the door shut angrily.

After latching the door, I pulled down my pants and sat on the toilet seat with my elbows propped up on my knees, panting in anger while I stared at the graffiti scrawled on the partition. Amidst a plethora of crude erection drawings showing them jetting their loads were a bunch of phone numbers with names to call for a 'good time'. I rolled my eyes as my bladder began to relax and when my stream started to spray into the toilet bowl, I heaved a sigh of relief, happy to empty my bladder and have some privacy while I did my business. But when I felt the last drops dribble out of my hanging appendage and I reached over to the side wall to grab a sheet of toilet paper to wipe my helmet, I suddenly heard some panting sounds coming from the cubicle next to mine.

I angled my eyebrows, thinking it was someone trying to empty his bowels, but as I pulled up my pants to exit my stall, I heard the man's vocalizations shift to a decidedly different kind of noise. Before long, the grunting turned into moaning, and as I paused my hand over the lock on my door, I hesitated while I held my breath to listen to him more closely. When I heard the distinctive fapping sound of the man jerking his cock in the echoing chamber, a small smile flitted over my lips while my jeans tightened around my crotch as my own organ started to twitch and swell.

"Fuck it," I whispered to myself, pulling down my pants again and sitting over my cold toilet seat.

Normally, I would have unrolled multiple sheets of toilet paper from the dispensary stapled to the side wall and folded them carefully over the seat so my bare skin wouldn't come anywhere near the filthy commode, but in this case I was too worked up to think about it. As my dick started to thicken and rise between my legs while I listened to the adjacent patron jerking his tool and groaning more loudly, I grasped my hard-on with two hands and lay back while I stroked it equally fast and hard.

"Suck on *this*, assholes," I grunted while I peered at my thick instrument popping in and out of my hands. "I'll show you a worm the likes of which you've never seen before..."

While I stroked my pole faster, causing the toilet seat to creak, the sound of the guy jerking off next to me suddenly stopped while silence filled the space between our two cubicles. After a few moments, I heard the sound of strange scratching against our shared partition, and I squinted at an unusual chrome plate affixed to the wall a few inches beside the toilet roll holder at waist height. I hadn't noticed it at first, thinking it was part of the normal fixtures, but when it started to wobble slightly, I saw that the lower bolt holding it to the wall was loose, and I leaned over to press my finger on the latch to keep it secure.

But when I felt a tap coming from the other side of the plate, I wrinkled my forehead and pulled out the bolt, watching the disc-shaped piece of metal swinging from side to side. I flipped it upwards a few inches, and when I saw a large gap cut between our wall with a shadow moving in the space next to me, I quickly let go of the covering, watching it swing from side to side while I caught my breath. Someone had gone to a great deal of effort to fashion some kind of hidden glory hole between the two compartments, and as my heart pounded in my chest, I peered down at my cock watching it bounce excitedly in my lap while it emitted a soft drop of precum out of the tip.

"Hey," a soft voice called from the other side. "Don't be

nervous, it's just us two guys getting off in the boy's room. I'll show you mine if you show me yours."

I paused for a long moment, alternately frightened and exhilarated at the prospect of jerking off in a public restroom with the guy in the next-door cubicle watching me, then I slowly lifted the latch, inserting the loose bolt into a small hole drilled on the upper edge to prop it open. The hole was a perfect circle, about six inches in diameter, with a rubber sleeve attached to the inner perimeter to protect against sharp edges. I lowered my head a few inches to peer into the next-door compartment, and when I saw the man's hard-on sticking straight up between his legs, I yanked my head back up, holding my hand over my mouth.

Holy shit! I thought to myself. *That guy is huge! He's even bigger than me, and my cock is nothing to sneeze at—at least when fully erect.*

I could feel him staring at my bobbing pole, and while I sat there frozen in fear, I suddenly heard him stroking his erection again, with the telltale slapping of his hand against his upper thighs.

"It's cool, man," the guy whispered while he stroked his hard-on. "We're alone now. Let me see you jerk that beautiful hard-on of yours. I like how you shaved your pubic hair, that's hot."

"Thanks," I whispered softly, not wanting to reveal my high feminine voice and show that I was actually a ladyboy using the men's washroom.

From his slightly elevated perspective, sitting a few feet inward from the hole in the wall, he couldn't see clearly between my slightly parted legs, so he wouldn't have noticed that I had a dripping slit where a man's balls would normally be. For now, at least, I was happy to continue the fabrication that we were simply two horny truckers stopping at the local diner for some harmless fun. I reached out to circle my throbbing instrument, and as I began to pump my hands up and down over my dripping pole, the guy next to me hummed in approval.

"Yes," he grunted while he jerked his erection in synchronicity with mine. "Pump that dick with two hands. That's a magnificent hard-on..."

"Thanks," I whispered, not wanting to get into a long discourse while we whispered pillow talk between the steel partition.

"Your hands are soft and smooth," he groaned as he slapped his hands harder over his parted thighs. "I'd love to feel them on my dick."

"Mmm," I grunted, not willing to escalate our impromptu encounter to the something more direct and intimate. "Come on my balls. I want to watch you spray your spunk on me."

"Fuck yes," the man grunted urgently. "I'm almost there. Oh *fuck*–"

Suddenly, he stood up and thrust his shaking erection through the hole in the partition, spraying his semen all over my legs while he groaned and shook his body against the trembling wall. For some reason, I found this brazen display of public sex highly stimulating, and within seconds, I was spraying my own spunk high into the air, commingling our cum as jets of semen flew all over the inside of my compartment.

It took me quite a while to finish coming, and when we both stopped dribbling, the man next to me kept his hard-on stuck through the portal while he panted heavily.

"That was fucking awesome," he hissed. "Are you up for a little more playtime? Because if you want to suck me or have me return the favor, I think I've got a little extra juice in the tank."

"Thanks," I whispered in a husky voice. "But I should get back on the road. I've got a delivery to make, and I'm running a bit late. Thanks for the show. That should get me the rest of the way to my destination."

"Anytime, sweetheart," the man purred, retracting his dripping tool from the hole and zipping up his pants before exiting his cubicle and stomping out of the restroom.

2

———

I paused for a moment, shocked at what I'd just done, then I peered down at my stained blouse for the first time, widening my eyes. I had no idea how I'd be able to exit the rest room gracefully in my disheveled state, but I couldn't stay here all day. After the stains began to dry, I stood up and removed my blouse, then I turned it inside out and put it back on, noticing they hadn't soaked all the way through. It felt gross to have my own and someone else's cum sticking against my skin, but when I heard the last person leave the restroom, I quickly left my cubicle and made my way back to my car. I tore open my suitcase and pulled out a dark sweater, then I unzipped the toiletry case and removed a travel-size pack of wet wipes, cleaning myself up as well as I could from inside the cover of my car.

When I saw the two assholes who'd flanked me at the urinal walking across the far end of the parking lot and driving off in their trucks, I breathed a sigh of relief, leaning against the wheel while I shook my head. I suddenly realized how hungry I'd become after my long drive, and my grumbling stomach reminded me there were some other bodily functions that needed my attention. I shoved the pack of wet wipes into my purse and headed back into the main lounge of the diner, taking a big breath of air. The greasy food of a truck stop wasn't exactly my first choice for a roadside meal, but it would have to do for now.

When I entered the restaurant, I found an open table near the window, ordering a club sandwich and a Coke. There were quite a few truckers sitting in the restaurant, mostly alone, and as I waited for my food, I scanned the room quietly. I'd pictured most long-haul truckers as middle-aged guys with pot bellies, but to my surprise, quite a few of them looked young and fit, even somewhat hunky. I studied them as they came and went, noticing quite a few availed themselves of the restroom before going on their way. But the longer I watched their movements, the more obvious a regular pattern became. I noticed some of them would glance around the room, and when they made eye contact with someone who met their gaze, they would nod silently at one another, then depart shortly thereafter to go to the men's restroom. After fifteen minutes or so, they would exit the cafe one after the other, with noticeable bulges in their pants, and drive off in their separate trucks.

So they don't just come here to eat after all, I smiled, watching two more guys heading toward the restroom.

The more I watched this fascinating dance of clandestine activity, the more stimulated I became after my exciting experience in the glory hole compartment. Before long, my hardening dick was pressing uncomfortably down the inside of jeans, demanding some immediate attention of its own. When I noticed a thirty-something guy with curly blond hair eyeing me over from the opposite corner of the diner, I offered a half-smile, then peered out the window, trying to ignore him. From all appearances–at least from the waist up–I looked like a full-blooded woman, and he couldn't have expected me to meet him for a private rendezvous in the men's restroom. But what he didn't know was that I had no hesitation about using the men's room when it fit my purposes, and this was definitely one of those times.

When he finished his meal and got up to head toward the washroom, I noticed him nodding at another patron as he passed by. But before the other guy even had a chance to wipe his face and finish his coffee, I quickly rose from my table and followed the blond hunk to the restroom. When I saw him enter the same cubicle I'd used earlier, I entered the stall next to his, quietly closing the door. I heard a shuffling sound coming from his compartment, then the familiar sound of the metal plate sliding open on the other side. I pulled down my pants and twisted the cover on my side upward, glancing into the open space. The blond guy already had his pants down over his knees with his cock pointing straight up. Within seconds, my own cock was hard as a rock.

"Hey man," he whispered, not wasting any time. "Do you like to give or receive?"

"Um–" I stammered, not expecting such an abrupt proposition. Reticent about sticking my dick through a metal hole with a stranger on the other side, I cleared my throat and lowered my voice to pretend I was a man. "Receive," I whispered curtly.

Within seconds, a big, throbbing hard-on poked through the hole, and I stared at it like it was some kind of alien. Pink colored and engorged with veins, it curled slightly upward while it bobbed softly, as if asking me to touch it. I hesitated for a moment, unsure whether to use my hands or my mouth, but his swelling bulb with a small drop of pre-cum on its slit drew my head unconsciously forward. Normally, I wouldn't suck a guy's cock who I didn't know at least informally, but there was something about this skanky arrangement that I found to be a huge turn-on. Whether it was the anonymity of the hookup or the slightly dirty idea of banging out a quickie in a public restroom that appealed to me, I couldn't be sure. Either way, I hadn't been this hard in a long time, and as I extended my tongue to lap up the cum sliding over his glans, the blond guy groaned in appreciation.

"Fuck, yes," he grunted. "Flick your tongue over my head. That feels so good..."

"Mmm," I groaned, closing my lips around his corona and sucking his organ into my mouth.

"Huh!" the hunk gasped when he felt his dick slide into my cavity, and I hesitated for a moment, concerned that other people using the rest room might overhear us.

But as the sound of footsteps entering and leaving the lavatory continued at a predictable pace and I listened to the sound of flushing toilets from adjacent stalls, I lowered my head over his erection, feeling his tip tenting the side of my cheek while I tried to position myself over my toilet seat. The whole thing seemed incredibly seedy, especially with the smell of people's bodily functions floating around the room, but this only heightened my excitement. I'd never done anything so spontaneous and risky in my entire life, and at this moment, I felt more alive than ever.

His dick tasted a bit salty and I had no idea what I would do when he came, but there was no way I was going to stop before we finished our impromptu affair. As he began to pump his dick into my eager mouth, I slid one hand through the bottom of the hole and cupped his balls, squeezing them softly.

"Oh God, yes," the guy huffed, pushing his manhood deeper into my mouth. "Squeeze my balls. I'm going to come soon. That's perfect."

Not wanting to miss one moment of the experience, I wrapped my other hand around his shaft as he pumped his erection in and out of the hole, and when I felt his pole beginning to pulse, I closed my eyes while he filled my mouth with his warm, salty cum. I held my lips over his pulsating organ while he shot seven jets into my cavity, then I paused as he panted on the other side of the partition, feeling his glans throbbing in my mouth. When he slowly retracted his dripping hard-on from my mouth, I leaned over and dribbled his semen into my toilet bowl, wiping the side of my mouth with the back of my hand. I might have enjoyed giving a stranger head in a seedy truck stop washroom, but there was no way I was going to swallow some guy's cum who'd I'd never met before.

"Thanks, man," the blond guy said from the other side as I heard him zipping up his pants and unlatching the lock on his cubicle door.

I definitely was more than ready for him to return the favor, and I chuckled when he slammed the door behind him, realizing these incognito trysts didn't follow the normal rules of sexual etiquette. These were more of a wham-bam-thank-you-ma'am kind of encounter, whereas soon as you got your rocks off, you got the hell out of there as soon as you could. This was poles apart from the usual romantic interlude, where each partner was careful to give the other person equal attention and ensure their physical needs were thoroughly met.

But I definitely had some needs that needed immediate attention. After I heard the blond hunk leave the restroom, I leaned back and grabbed my erection with both hands, watching it pump through my fingers as my face flushed in excitement. I would have preferred to have someone sucking me right now, but I was so turned on from the brief illicit hookup that I could have come from rubbing my dick against the cold steel wall. But just as I was about to pop off, I heard someone enter the stall next to me and I glanced over at the partition, realizing that I'd left the cover to the glory hole open. Within seconds, someone's mouth stuck through the gap, with his tongue waving in circles as he smiled at my upturned dick.

"Nice cock, man," the guy said, sliding his tongue sensuously over his lips. "Do you want some help with that? I could use a little milkshake to go with my burger."

I paused for a moment, taken aback by his crude come-on, then I pulled my hands away from my throbbing organ, chuckling softly.

I guess I wouldn't have to wait so long for some oral satisfaction after all.

3

—————

I raised up from my toilet seat so he couldn't see that I was a hermaphrodite, then when he pulled his face away from the hole, I stuck my dick through the opening and he hungrily wolfed it all the way down his throat. I was taken aback at first by the sensation of having my entire pole massaged orally, but as my labia slapped against the man's chin, I closed my eyes, savoring his technique. It was obvious that many people visited this truck stop as professional cocksuckers, and I had no problem at all with availing myself of his expert services. But when he reached into the hole to fondle my balls, suddenly he pulled his head away in dismay.

"What the hell, man?" he said. "Are you a *lady*?"

"Well," I purred in my usual feminine voice. "I'm more of a lady-*boy*."

"You're not like any ladyboy *I've* ever known," he said, staring at my dripping lips and my bobbing cock through the hole.

"I'm a special kind of ladyboy. One with both girl and boy parts. You don't like?"

"Oh, I like, alright," he grinned, reaching out to slide his fingers over my slippery labia. "It's just that I've never fucked a real hermaphrodite before."

"Well, I guess today's your lucky day. Were you going to finish giving me head or just stare at my dick all day long?"

"Fuck, yes," he grunted, sticking his chin back through the opening. "Fuck my face with that beautiful ladyboy cock. I want to feel you gushing down my hole."

"Mmm, I like the sound of that," I said, slapping my hard-on against the side of his face as my pre-cum splashed over his cheeks.

He swiped his tongue from side-to-side trying to catch my drops, then I thrust my poker into his mouth, ramming it all the way to the hilt. Normally, I wouldn't be so rough with my partners, but it was obvious this guy had done this plenty of times before and obviously enjoyed deep-throating anyone who wanted a quick toss. When he slipped two fingers into my pussy and curled them upwards toward my prostate gland, I moaned softly, feeling the familiar tingling in my lower groin.

"Yes, baby," I grunted, looking for something to hold onto while I slapped my hips against the shaking cubicle parti-tion. "Massage my G-spot like that. I'm going to cum all the way down your throat any second now..."

"Mmm," the guy on the other side nodded while he squeezed my dick harder with his throat muscles.

"Oh fuck," I gasped, holding onto the top of the wall with both hands while I tensed my buttock muscles and pushed my pulsating organ hard against his dripping mouth. *"Yesssss..."*

When he felt me coming down his throat, he moaned along with me, holding me tightly until I'd expelled every last drop of my spunk. I paused for a moment, panting against the cold metal wall while I savored the feeling of my dick throbbing in his throat, then he pulled back a few inches, tightening his lips while he sucked the last vestiges of my semen oozing out of the tip of my crown. When my hard-on popped out of his mouth, he kissed the glistening tip gently, then he rolled his tongue over his lips to catch the final drips of my dew, sucking them sweetly into his mouth.

"Damn, you're good at that," I panted, glancing down at my throbbing organ like he had literally sucked all the blood from the rest of my body directly toward my swelling tool.

"Well, I've had quite a bit of practice," he smiled, still resting on his knees on the opposite side of the partition.

"I bet you have," I chuckled, noticing his upturned willie pointing up in his lap. "Now, what can I do for you?"

"Normally, I'm happy just to *receive* in these situations," the man said. "But there's something about your ladyboy pussy that reminds me of gay sex. I don't suppose you'd let me–"

"Fuck me from behind?" I grinned, finishing his thought.

"Actually, I was thinking more from the *front*, if you think you can manage it. I'd love to play with your cock at the same time I'm fucking you. I like to watch my partners squirt when we make love..."

"I might be able to work something out," I said, peering at the graffiti scrawled on the wall above the glory hole cutout. "Give me a moment to get arranged, and I'll be right with you."

"No worries," the guy chuckled while he stroked his erection gently from the other side. "My dick isn't going anywhere."

I reached into my purse and pulled out my pack of wet wipes, placing it atop the water tank on top of my commode.

I pulled out a few sheets and wiped them thoroughly over the stained partition before throwing them in my toilet basin. Then I removed one last cloth, poking a hole in the middle with my fingernail and placing it over the tip of my hard-on and pulling it down over the base until the moist towelette rested over the top of my mound and my dripping labia.

"I guess this will have to do for now," I smiled, moving my hips closer to the hole. "I hope you don't mind fucking me while I wear a safety bib. I'm not too thrilled about rubbing my pussy against this grungy restroom wall."

"It's a bit unconventional," the man laughed, peering at the strange umbrella-shaped contraption through the gap in the wall. "But as long as I've got a clear point of access to your pussy, I suppose it doesn't matter what else is in the way."

"Okay," I said, grabbing hold of my right knee and pulling it upward while I clasped the back of my ankle and pressing it against the partition.

I pushed my hips forward, feeling the tension in the back of my thighs slowly beginning to dissipate until my foot rested near the top of the wall with my legs angled upright in a perfect one-hundred-and-eighty-degree split.

"Good thing I practice this position in my yoga class every week," I chuckled, angling my cock through the hole while I positioned my vulva over the center of the gap.

My crudely constructed hygiene barrier flapped under my pussy, offering a modicum of protection against the gritty surface of the wall, then I tapped the side of the wall with my fingers, indicating that I was ready.

"We better do this before I pull a muscle or something," I said. "I'm not used to making out in such close quarters."

"No worries," the man said, raising up his body and

poking his dick through the hole. "I don't imagine this will take very long. I haven't been this turned on since–well, since I was with my *first* ladyboy."

"Can you reach me alright in this position?" I said, glancing down at his smaller-than-normal-sized dick.

"I think so," he said, raising the lower half of the improvised wet wipe upward while he tilted his hips forward.

When I felt the tip of his cock enter my cavity, I pushed my hips further forward to make a tight seal against the wall, then the man on the other side of the wall groaned when he felt his dick sink into my wet cavity.

"Better?" I said, feeling him squeeze my upturned erection on the other side of the partition while he titled his hips upward.

"Better," he moaned, rocking his hips gently.

"Be careful," I panted as he began to jerk my cock while he rocked his hips back and forth. "We haven't got a lot of room to work with, and I'd hate to lose the connection."

"Yeah," he huffed, jerking his hips awkwardly against the shaking partition. "I'm sorry I'm not as big as some other guys."

"No, it's not that," I lied, flexing my ass as I struggled to keep my hips joined against his. "It's just a bit of an uncomfortable position, and I don't know how much longer I can hold it..."

"You won't need to," the man huffed. "I'm getting close. Your pussy feels so warm and wet–"

"Warmer and wetter than the *other* holes you're used to plowing?" I smiled.

"Definitely," he grunted.

I tightened my fingers over the top of the partition wall, feeling the pleasure gradually rising in my pumping cock. Although the man's dick was barely long enough to penetrate my opening, whatever he was doing with his hands on the opposite side was more than making up for the lack of stimulation on my side.

"I'm going to come soon if you keep stroking me like that," I warned him.

"Yes, please," he hissed as he stared down at the widening slit on top of my crown. "I can't wait to see you squirting all over my belly."

"Unghh," I groaned, feeling my dick beginning to pulse as my semen shot up my pole. *"Gahhh..."*

"Holy shit," the other guy huffed, slapping his hips hard against the partition while I creamed over his stomach. "Fuck, fuck, fuck–"

I could tell from the rhythm of his panting that he was coming inside me, and as he gripped my pulsating hard-on tightly in his hands, he angled his balls upward, emptying his load inside my pussy while we both groaned in satisfaction. When I felt him begin to relax his hips from the other side, I pulled my pussy from the front of the hole and lowered my aching legs, trying to catch my breath.

"Sorry for the rapid decoupling," I said, massaging the back of my thighs while I sat over the toilet seat, pushing his jism into the bowl. "My legs were beginning to hurt from being stretched in that position, and I needed to rest."

"No problem," the other guy said. "That wasn't near as fast as *most* guys in this place pull out. They're usually in a hurry to disappear as soon as they finish coming."

"I guess I'm not like most guys," I laughed.

"You certainly aren't," the man chuckled. "Thank you for this very unexpected and very satisfying liaison. I enjoyed that far more than most of these encounters."

"It was my pleasure," I nodded, pulling the jerry-rigged

condom off the top of my dripping hard-on and throwing it in the toilet bowl.

"Maybe I'll see you around if you're traveling this way again," he said, pulling up his pants and beginning to unlatch his door.

"Not likely," I said, noticing a line of shadows under the bottom of my door as the guy with the little cock exited the compartment.

Within seconds, another man immediately entered the cubicle, pulling down his trousers and pushing his dick through the hole.

It looks like I'm getting a bit of a reputation around here, I chuckled to myself, glancing at the graffiti on the wall. Maybe I'll have to add my number to the list of good time hookups before I leave this truck stop.

4

"Whoa, big boy!" I chuckled, abandoning any further attempt to disguise my voice. "Aren't we getting a little ahead of ourselves?"

"I dunno," the guy on the other side of the partition said. "It sounds like you've been keeping pretty busy servicing guys from your side of the wall."

"Maybe so," I huffed. "But a girl has needs too."

"What did you have in mind?" the man said. "I'm up for just about anything..."

"So I can see," I smiled, staring at his bobbing hard-on poking through the hole in the wall. His dick was fair-sized, but not as long and thick as mine, and when I stuck my pole through the gap next to his, he gasped.

"Nice cock," he grunted. "That's pretty big for a tranny."

"I'm not technically a *tranny*," I corrected him. "Take a look at my balls and you'll see what I mean."

The guy pulled his cock out of the hole for a moment, and when I heard him bend down to stare at my equipment, he gasped.

"Holy shit," the man said. "How did you manage to do

that? That must have been some expensive surgery you had–"

"Not at all," I said. "I was *born* this way. It doesn't happen very often, but when it does, it's a sight to behold."

"I'll say," the man said, falling down onto his knees to glance at my organs more closely. "Do you mind if I *lick* it?"

"Which part?" I laughed, feeling my juices dripping out of my wet slit and my flaring crown at the same time. "My *girl* part or my *boy* part?"

"Both," he said, extending his tongue toward the base of my dick. "I've never sucked a *real* ladyboy before."

"Have at it, baby," I nodded, tilting my hips upward to give him freer access to my dripping vulva. "It feels good either way."

Within seconds, I felt his tongue pressing between my folds while he grasped my bobbing shaft with one hand, stroking me firmly as he slurped and sucked my snatch. I chuckled at his awkward technique, realizing that without a regular clitoris, he wasn't sure where to target his attention. But what he didn't know was that my boy-cock was simply an oversize extension of my clit, and that I had just as much sensitive erectile tissue *inside* my pussy, just like every other woman.

"Mmm, yes," I purred as I held onto the top of the metal dividing panel for support. "Fuck me with your tongue. That feels good. Do you like jerking my big ladyboy dick?"

"Mm-hmm," he nodded enthusiastically, sucking my labia into his mouth as he probed my cavity with his tongue.

"Did you know that intersex girls like me can come both ways?" I teased while I watched his glistening face licking up my juices. "We can squirt out of both our dicks and our pussies. Would you like to see that?"

"Mm-hmm," he grunted, squeezing my dick harder while he rammed his face harder into my cunt.

"Curl your tongue upwards a bit," I coached him. "I've got a G-spot, just like every other girl. If you want to make me gush all over your face, you've got to stimulate me in the right place..."

The guy tilted his head a bit to the side to get better leverage, then he yanked my dick downward like he was operating a stick-shift, causing my pussy to tilt directly over the tip of his probing tongue.

"Yeah, baby," I hissed, closing my eyes in pleasure while I felt my pussy tenting open in pleasure, preparing to squeeze down hard at the moment of climax. "Just like that. Don't stop..."

"Uh-uh," he murmured, waiting for me to come all over his face.

"Oh fuck," I groaned, feeling myself passing the point of no return. "Here it comes, baby. I'm gonna cum so hard–"

When my orgasm washed over me, I felt my pussy lips clamping open and shut in powerful contractions while I shot my load high over his shaking head, landing on his back and tightly gripping hand. At the same time, my Skene's gland shot out its contents, gushing its juices over his face while I thrashed and moaned against the shaking partition. At this point, I didn't even care who might be listening, since my little secret had likely spread around the entire restaurant as a lineup of horny dudes queued up outside my door.

"Holy fuck," the man panted when I finished spraying my ladyboy juices all over his face and head. "That was insane. I have got to get me some more of this. I haven't been this hard since I was a teenager and I found my dad's porn stash."

"Oh yeah?" I smiled. "Do you want to stick your dipstick into my reservoir? Because there's a lot more where that came from..."

"Fuck, yes," the man grunted, standing up next to the dripping hole and sticking his throbbing hard-on through the hole. "Give me some of that hot ladyboy pussy."

I stared at his dick for a moment, then I peered at my package of wet wipes resting on top of the toilet bowl, shaking my head. The last thing I wanted to do was improvise some kind of hygiene barrier again between the two of us while I wiggled my ass against the filthy wall.

"Why don't you come over to my side this time?" I said. "We can do this far more comfortably if you're sitting in my lap."

I don't think I heard a guy zip up his pants so quickly in my whole life as he scrambled to put on his clothes and exit his cubicle.

"Excuse me," I heard him mutter as he squeezed in front of the other guys waiting in line to have a turn at me. "This won't take long."

I unlatched the lock on my door, and when he quickly slipped inside my stall, I noticed a row of peeping Toms leaning over to catch a glimpse of my curvy figure and shiny cock before he closed the door behind him.

"Why the hurry?" I smiled at the trucker, much younger and cuter than I imagined from the other side of the wall. "We've got all afternoon in the privacy of our own little cubicle."

"Those guys are practically *foaming at the mouth*," he said, tilting his head toward my closed door. "I don't think we've got very long before they break down the front door."

"I'm sure they won't mind *listening* for a while," I grinned, noticing the shadows under the gap of my door becoming thicker and more restless. "It will just get them more in the mood for when their time comes."

As the man nodded and quickly unzipped his trousers, I couldn't help but chuckle quietly to myself. When I came here to relieve myself, I hadn't planned on becoming the main attraction at the roadside pit stop, but I was happy to milk it for as long as it lasted.

5

When the guy pulled out his dick and stood in front of me with it flapping in front of my face, I think he half-expected me to suck it right there. But the last thing I wanted was to be a revolving dick whore, so I peered up at him and smiled softly.

"Surely we can be a little more creative than *that*," I said. "Don't you want to try something new for a change?"

"Um, sure," he said, staring at my curvy breasts darting the front of my sweater and my glistening cock, bouncing gently over the front of the toilet seat. "Do you want to do it sitting down or standing up?"

"I wouldn't mind sitting this time," I nodded. "Why don't we switch places while I rest on your lap? That way, you can play with my cock while you fuck me from behind."

"That works for me," the guy grinned as his erection flapped through his zipper.

I got up from the toilet and we awkwardly shifted positions in the tight compartment, brushing our bodies together while we streaked slippery lines of cum over each other's bellies from our pointed erections. When he sat down on the seat and spread his legs apart, displaying his upturned hard-on, I turned around and slowly bent over at the waist, displaying my glistening pussy inches away from his face.

"Oh my God," he groaned, barely believing his luck finding a hot ladyboy in this secret hookup spot instead of the usual greasy trucker just looking to get his rocks off.

"Do you like?" I grinned, sliding two fingers up the back of his pole while his legs trembled in anticipation.

"Fuck, yes," he grunted, pressing his head forward and burying his face between my cheeks.

He grasped the sides of my ass and extended his tongue, lapping up the juices dribbling out of my slit, then I angled my hips upward a few inches.

"That feels good," I purred. "But do you know what feels even *better*? When you lick my butthole."

He hesitated for a moment with his nose in my crack, then I chuckled softly while I squeezed the tip of his throbbing tool.

"Don't worry," I said. "It's all shaved and squeaky-clean down there. We girls like to keep things neat and tidy in our silk panties."

I bent over a little further and spread my cheeks apart to show him my pink rosebud, and he audibly gasped, flaring his eyes open as stared as my pretty pucker.

"Haven't you seen one of those before?" I teased while I stroked his bobbing erection with the tips of my fingers. "Surely you've watched PornHub a few times–"

"Yes," he said. "But usually it's straight hetero action, where most of the focus is on the girl's pussy and tits."

"Well, you should change your search words once in a while. It's a singular pleasure watching a girl with a sweet ass jilling herself, especially when she's lying upside down.

When she climaxes, you can actually see her pucker spasming with each contraction..."

"Really?" the guy said, sliding his finger through my parted crease and pausing over my tingling sphincter. "I had no idea–"

"Why don't you try it for *yourself*?" I smiled. "Lick my ring while you jerk my dick from the other side. I'll tell you when I'm about to come so you can have a front-row seat for the entire spectacle."

"What about–?"

"Don't worry," I chuckled. "I promise to make it worth your while. I'll let you sink your willie deep into my *other* hole right after I pop off. How often do you get a chance to lick a ladyboy's ass and stroke her dick while you fuck her at the same time?"

"Shit, yes," he grunted, reaching around to squeeze my dick with both hands while he pulled my ass against his face, sliding his tongue over my anus while I rocked my hips over the toilet seat.

It took him a while to get in the rhythm of jerking my cock from behind while he licked my ass with his tongue, but after a few minutes, he got totally into it, twisting his tongue like a pit viper over my starfish while I pumped my dick in his hands. As I felt my pleasure slowly rising from his expert technique, I raised my flushed face to peer at the front door of my cubicle, noticing a row of stacked heads peering at me through the thin cracks on the side of the panel.

So much for having a little privacy while you do your business, I chuckled to myself while I grinned at the crowd of peeping Toms. *If they want a show while they wait for their turn, I better give them a good one.*

I reached up to pull off my sweater, then I unclasped my

bra and hung my garments over the hook holding my purse on the back of the door. When the rubberneckers saw my pretty tits bouncing on my chest while the guy behind me pumped my dick with his hands, I could hear their murmurs as their mouths gaped open and they nodded their heads excitedly.

"Yes, baby," I grunted, becoming even more turned on by the lusty audience watching us from the other side of the door. "I'm almost there. Stick your tongue in my hole to put me over the edge. I can feel it coming–"

Much to my surprise, the guy didn't hesitate to dart the tip of his tongue and stick it a few inches into my tight tunnel as I felt the pressure building to the bursting point. When I felt the taps release, I pulled my butt away from his face, and groaned loudly while I squirted six hard jets of cum toward the front of my door panel while the observers blinked and moaned along with me. I could feel my butt clamping in hard spasms while my dick pulsed in the guy's hands and his hot breath billowed over my quivering butt cheeks, then just when he thought the show couldn't possibly get any better, I pressed my hips down over his dripping hard-on, slipping his erection all the way into my still-pulsing pussy.

He was already too far gone to control himself any longer, and when he felt his dick embedded in my warm, slippery pocket, he groaned in delirious ecstasy, emptying his load deep into my cavity. I kept coming for a little longer, watching my ropes of semen arching upwards and dropping onto the floor in decreasing arcs until I was completely spent, slumping forward over my knees while the guy behind me pulsed his last few spasms of pleasure in my dripping pussy.

"So, what do you think?" I said to him while I rested over his throbbing cock. "Did you enjoy the show?"

"That was the hottest thing I've ever seen," he nodded, squeezing my tits softly while he slowly relaxed his leg muscles. "It wasn't just your *butthole* that was contracting when you came. Your entire pelvic floor was pulsating when I felt you shoot into my hands."

"It's a beautiful thing, isn't it?" I grinned. "The next time you're wondering if your girlfriend is faking it, just watch her sphincter when she climaxes. If you see her little starfish puckering, you'll know it's legit."

"Got it," the guy nodded as he pinched my nipples. "Something tells me I'll be spending a lot more time down there from now on."

6

When my back-door lover got up to exit the cubicle, he opened the front door and there was a sudden commotion as those standing next to the door struggled to see who would squeeze into the compartment next. When two guys finally managed to slip in between the swirling throng, they hastily closed the door and latched it shut while the others pounded on it from the other side. I peered up at them as they looked at one another with wrinkled foreheads, wondering what the hell they would do now.

"Is this a tag-team operation?" I chuckled, darting my eyebrows. "Or do you guys *always* go to the toilet together?"

"Sorry about that," the first guy panted, trying to catch his breath after fighting off the rest of the competing paramours. "We kind of both got pushed in here unexpectedly..."

"Well, it looks like you're stuck for the time-being," I said. "If one of you tries to squeeze out now, you're likely to let the entire crowd in. And there's barely enough room for two of us in here as it is."

"What do you say?" the first guy said to the second one,

looking at him uncertainly. "Rock, paper, scissors to see who goes first? I don't mind watching while I wait my turn–"

"Who says you have to *wait your turn*?" I smiled. "There's no reason why you both can't get your jollies at the same time. I'm guessing this isn't the first time you've found yourself dick to dick in a place like this before."

"Ah, that might be able to work," the second guy said, nodding toward his unwelcome companion.

I glanced at the bulges in their pants and chuckled with a sly grin.

"You're used to sucking other men's cocks through the *glory hole*, right?" I said while I twisted my fingers over my flagging tool as I sat on the toilet seat with my legs slightly parted. "How about if you put on a little show for me to get me back in the mood?"

"I'm usually the one *getting* sucked, not giving it," the first guy said.

"Same here," his partner nodded.

"Well, you certainly seemed to be in a hurry to get your hands on *this* one," I grinned, slapping my semi-tumescent dick against the inside of my glistening thighs. "If you suck one cock, it's pretty much like any other..."

The two guys glanced at one another nervously, with neither one willing to make the first move.

"I'm not expecting you to *swallow* it, for crying out loud," I said. "Just give me a little bit of mutual fellatio, and I'll make it worth your while. After all, I've got a whole lot more to work with."

The two guys glanced at my erect nipples and the glistening slit between my legs, then the first one slowly squatted down onto his knees.

"Alright," he said to the second guy. "As long as you promise not to come in my mouth."

"Don't worry," the other dude said. "I plan on saving that for the main attraction. This is just a *warm-up*."

The first one grabbed the tip of the other guy's tool between his two fingers, then he slowly pointed the bobbing hard-on toward his mouth, flicking his tongue tentatively over the dripping head.

"Yeah," the second guy panted. "Swirl your tongue around the tip of my cock. That feels good..."

The first guy hesitated for a moment, then he turned his head slightly to the side, rolling his tongue over the base of his new friend's swelling corona while the other guy rocked his hips gently.

"Fuck yes," the second guy groaned, tilting his head downward while he watched his partner make love to his cock. "Just like that."

"See?" I chuckled as I watched the two men rocking their bodies together. "It's not so bad, after all. It's kind of like sucking a freshly grilled hot dog. A nice warm, *juicy* hot dog..."

"Mmm," the first guy murmured as he slipped the other guy's dick into his mouth while he grabbed the shaft with one hand and slipped his other hand between his legs to squeeze his balls.

"Something tells me this isn't the first time you've done something like this," I smiled, feeling my dick starting to tingle as it slowly rose upward between my parted legs.

"Mmmft," the first guy nodded as his partner placed his hands behind his head and pumped his dick further into his mouth.

"Squeeze his balls harder," I nodded as I placed one hand around my dripping crown and watched my cum starting to drip out of my slit. "I know you guys like that. Now you're getting me turned on..."

The second guy twisted his head to glance at me, and when he saw that I had a glistening cleft where a guy's balls normally were positioned, his eyes flared open as he grunted loudly.

"Careful there, truckie," I smiled, tilting my hips upward so he could see my parted labia dripping fluid down the crease of my ass. "You better not get too excited lest you drop your load before it's delivered to its final destination."

"Yeah," he grunted, pulling his hard-on out of his partner's mouth and watching it bounce excitedly in front of his face as he panted heavily. "There's somewhere *else* I plan to sink my dick before I'm finished here."

"Okay," I said, jerking my hips upward to slap my partial erection over the front of my belly. "It's your turn now. Let's see if you can get me fully hard."

"Right," he said, peering at the first guy as they stood face-to-face with their dripping poles almost touching.

"I've got a better idea," I said, suddenly feeling new life in my surging erection. "I want to watch you guys rubbing your dicks together while you squeeze them in your hands. I always thought that was the hottest thing two guys could do to one another. There's nothing like watching two dudes creaming over each other's dicks while they frot them together."

"Okay..." the first guy said, slowly pressing his hips forward to position his prick over the other guy's and gripping their joined tools with both hands as he began to rock his hips forward. "But I think we might need a little lube, though. It's kind of dry and sticky right now–"

"Well, it's your lucky day," I grinned, lowering my hand between my legs to slide my fingers over my dripping slit. "I just happen to have an unlimited supply right here."

I reached out and swiped my slippery fingers over their

joined cocks while they shuddered in pleasure, then I nodded for them to continue.

"Will that work a little better?" I smiled.

"Much," the first guy nodded, glancing up at his partner's increasingly flushed face as they rocked their hips together and groaned softly.

"That's more like it," I said, watching their mouths gaping open while they both gripped their hands together over their reddening poles. "Now kiss each other while you jerk each other's dicks."

The first guy paused for a moment, suddenly twisting his head in my direction.

"I don't kiss dudes," he said.

"You will *today* if you want a piece of this," I said, swinging my hips while my erection tilted from side to side.

"Alright," he huffed. "Just this once. But you better be ready to put that thing to work pretty soon. Because I've got big plans for what I intend to do to you."

"I bet you do," I grinned, sticking two fingers deep into my slit while I rolled my other hand over my dripping glans. "Now, stick your tongue down your partner's throat while you rub your cocks together. It shouldn't be long now."

The two men paused for a moment, then when their lips met, they moaned in each other's mouths as the sound of wet, slapping flesh echoed around the compartment. As I slathered more of my juices over their joined cocks, they slowly inserted their tongues into each other's mouths, quickly forgetting that they weren't actually gay. I smiled as they began to pump their hips harder toward one another while they gripped their swelling dicks tightly, slapping their dripping crowns against one another's bellies as they grunted in rising pleasure. When the first guy suddenly starting squirting over the other guy's belly, the second one flung his eyes open in surprise, then he groaned loudly as his knees buckled and he moaned into his partner's mouth, jetting his spunk over their joined hands and dripping stomachs.

I waited until they both finished climaxing and pulled their heads back as their dicks bobbed excitedly in front of their glistening stomachs.

"Now that's what I call some hot man-on-man action," I nodded, feeling my own pre-cum sliding out of the tip of my bobbing hard-on and streaming down the sides of my pole. "Are you ready for some *girl-on-boy* action now, or are you too exhausted to continue?"

"Oh, I'm ready alright," the first guy said, turning around to face me as a long string of cum drizzled down onto the cubicle floor.

"Me too," the other guy grinned, squeezing in next to the first guy to get the first shot at me.

"There's no need to fight over it," I said, staring at their two bobbing erections. "There's plenty of me to go around. I think we might be able to find a way to keep you both entertained at the same time with a little creative positioning..."

7

"**W**hat were you thinking?" the first guy said as he ran his eyes up and down my naked figure. "Because I'd be happy to fuck you pretty much *anywhere...*"

"I was thinking of a different kind of frotting action this time," I smiled. "How would you like to fuck my pussy at the same time?"

"*DP?*" the second guy said, raising an eyebrow as he peered at his new friend. "I've always wanted to try that."

"I'm game if you are," the first guy nodded. "But how can we position ourselves in this narrow space to pull it off? I've done it lying down before, but that's not going to work in this small cubicle–"

I paused for a moment while I stared at their erections bouncing over their stomachs, then I nodded.

"Why don't we try standing in a sandwich position against the wall?" I said. "One of you can lean with your back against the partition while I mount you from the front, then the other can enter me from behind at the same time."

"When you say from *behind*," the second guy said. "Do you mean–"

"In my *pussy*," I chuckled. "You guys seem to like the feeling of rubbing your dicks together. Let's see how you like it with my warm snatch squeezing you this time."

"It works for me," the first guy nodded. "As long as I can get a piece of that pretty ladyboy pussy, I'm happy either way."

"So, now we just need to figure out who goes on the front and who goes on the back," I smiled. "There are certain advantages both ways–"

"If I take the front..." the first guy nodded. "I can play with your tits and your boy-cock while I fuck you."

"True," I said, turning my hips so both men could see the curvature of my ass. "But if you take me from *behind*, you get to feel my pretty ladyboy butt slapping against your belly while I gush all over your balls."

"Fuck," the first guy hissed, flaring his eyes open in excitement. "Since you put it that way–"

"Rock, paper, scissors?" the second guy chuckled.

"Winner takes the back?" the first guy said.

"Uh-huh."

"Okay," the first guy said, raising his fist in front of his stomach. "On the count of three. Ready?"

"Ready," the other guy said, bumping his fist against his partner's.

The two men pumped their fists together three times, then on the third count, they opened their hands with two different signs. The first one extended all of his fingers together in a smooth plane while the second one parted his index and middle fingers in the scissors position.

"Scissors beats paper," the second guy nodded.

"Two out of three?" the first guy said.

The second guy peered at the first one with a dubious expression, then he chuckled.

"Okay, but that's it," he said. "I'm ready to pump something softer and wetter than my hand in this stinky washroom."

The two men pumped their hands together for two more rounds, after which the first guy emerged the winner.

"Fuck!" the second guy huffed when he realized he lost. "I knew I should have stopped after the first round."

"Is it really so bad?" I said, rising up off my commode and rubbing my tits against the side of his body while I nibbled on his neck. "Wouldn't you like to *kiss* me when you fuck me?"

"Hey!" the first guy said, glaring at me angrily. "You didn't mention that was part of the deal earlier!"

"Too late now," I grinned, grabbing hold of the other guy's dick and swinging him against the opposite wall with a loud slap.

As he leaned against the partition with his hard-on pointed straight up, I pressed the front of my body against his, rising up on my toes to point his tip into my tingling opening. When I sank my body down over his erection, he groaned loudly, squeezing my tits and burying his face in my neck while he stared at my erection sliding up over his belly-button. When I lowered myself as far as I could, I felt the other guy moving behind me, then he slapped his tool against the sides of my ass, humming approvingly.

"That's a chick's *ass*, alright," he said. "Not like some of the other ladyboys I've seen in this place. I could fuck that all day..."

"Just make sure you put it in the right hole," I chuckled, turning around to glance over my shoulder while he stared greedily at my butt cheeks. "You'll like the *other* one better, anyhow. It's a whole lot tighter and wetter right now."

"Mmm," the first guy hummed as I arched my back for him to see my dripping pussy with the other guy's throbbing shaft firmly positioned inside me. "That's a sight I don't see very often."

He grabbed the end of his hard-on with two fingers and pointed it next to my hole, flexing his hips upward while trying to squeeze it into the opening, but he kept sliding off to one side and up the crack of my butt.

"Are you sure you don't want it from the *back side*?" he said, pushing his crown gently against my tightening sphincter. "It will be a whole lot easier this way–"

I turned around and grabbed his dick with one hand to deter him from getting any further ideas, then I raised up on my toes while lifting myself off the second guy's erection.

"Wait a moment," I said, thankful he hadn't rammed his cock into whatever hole was most convenient.

Then I reached between my thighs and grabbed hold of both of their poles, squeezing their heads together while I pointed them towards my slippery hole. When they felt the gap in my folds, they instinctively arched their hips upward at the same time, sliding their joined erections inside my burning tunnel.

"Is that better now?" I grinned as both men groaned in ecstasy.

"Fuck yes," the guy behind me said as he felt his organ sliding against the man in front, while I lowered my body down over both of their throbbing instruments.

"Better than frotting your friend's cock with your *hands*?"

"*Christ*, yes," he hissed, grabbing hold of the sides of my ass and beginning to hump me from behind.

"How about *you*, big boy?" I said to the second guy facing

me while I slithered my pointed tits over his hairy chest and pressed my hard dick against his rippled abs. "Are you *still* sorry you lost the competition?"

"Are you kidding me?" he said, placing his hands softly around the sides of my head and planting his lips against mine while his tongue probed me almost as deep as his dick was. "This is the hottest thing I've ever done, with a man or a woman."

"How about with one who's a little bit of *both*?" I moaned, slurping my tongue with his while the two men fucked me like it was the first time getting their dick wet.

"Damn straight," he nodded, reaching between our shaking bellies to place his hands around my rod and jerk it firmly while he slid his dick inside my tunnel against the man on the opposite side. "I feel like I've won the lottery."

"And you haven't even collected the main *prize* yet," I grinned, feeling the pressure starting to build in my abdomen toward a powerful climax.

"Oh, I'll be *collecting* it alright," he huffed as he squeezed my dick tighter. "I'll be making a sizable deposit any time now."

"Yes, baby," I groaned in his ear as I felt my flood gates starting to open. "Let me feel you both coming inside me. I can't hold it any longer..."

When I suddenly collapsed my weight over their joined poles and gushed my juices simultaneously out of the bottom of my slit and over the second guy's flexing abs, both men howled like timberwolves as they deposited their junk inside me, shaking their bodies together while they felt each other's shafts throbbing and pulsing together. We'd been making so much noise shaking the partition between the stalls that I hadn't even noticed that someone else had stuck his dick through the glory hole on the opposite side, jerking himself to climax while he listened and spied on the three of us having the most exciting threesome of our lives.

When we finally extricated ourselves from our trembling embrace, I glanced at the flushed faces and dripping erections of the two men, grinning like a Cheshire Cat.

"Are you still sorry you squeezed in here together?" I said to them.

"Not for a second," the first man said, glancing at the long streams of cum and lubrication dripping down the insides of my thighs. "That was a hundred times better than my typical solo encounter in this place. You give a whole new meaning to the term *glory hole*."

"Same here," the second guy said. "I don't know how it will ever be the same coming into this place for a quickie after this."

"Maybe you should try it the *old-fashioned* way next time," I laughed. "There's something to be said for feeling somebody's warm body next to you when you're making love to them."

"There certainly is," the first guy said, pinching my nipples softly as he pulled up his pants.

"Thanks, sweetheart," the second guy said, kissing me gently on the side of my cheek. "This is one truck stop rendezvous I'll never forget."

8

I peered at the row of flaring eyes staring at me through the crack of the front door to my cubicle and the shuffling sound of bodies in the stall next to mine as they struggled to get a glance at my ladyboy figure.

"Could you guys do me one last favor before you leave?" I asked the two men zipping up their pants.

"Anything," the first man said.

"Could you escort me out of this place when we exit the cubicle? I've had enough sex for one day, and I don't think my pussy can take any more pounding from these foaming dudes waiting at the gate. I could use two strong guys to keep them from jumping me before I go on my way."

"No worries," the first one said, nodding toward his accomplice. "How about if I go first and clear the way while you follow behind the girl to make sure nobody molests her?"

"Good plan," the second guy said, pulling me between their two bodies after I finished putting on my clothes and retrieved my purse from the back of the door.

When they unlatched the lock, it suddenly pushed

inward as a swarm of bodies tumbled over one another, struggling to get into the compartment.

"Back off!" the first guy said, raising up his elbows in front of his chest like a snowplow. "The lady is done with her business here. Let us out or someone is going to get seriously hurt!"

The crowd slowly backed off and parted when they saw that my two escorts meant business, and we slowly inched our way out of the jammed hall while huddled together until we finally got out into the parking lot and some fresh air.

"Thanks, guys," I said, realizing that I hadn't even bothered to ask the names of any of my impromptu lovers in the rest stop hookup. "I appreciate everything you've done for me. Especially treating me like a *lady* and not some tramp you found in a dirty truck stop."

"It was our pleasure," the first man said, clasping my hand and kissing it softly. "There's no doubt that you're a lady, even if you *do* have a little extra decoration. But that only makes you all the more desirable."

"Are you okay making it the rest of the way alone?" the second man said, glancing around him to make sure no other truckers were having second thoughts about grabbing me.

"My car is just over there," I nodded, tilting my head toward my white SUV. "I've got it from here."

"Well, if you ever need some extra company or a free bodyguard," the first guy said, pulling a card out of his wallet. "Give me a call anytime."

"Same here," the second guy said, handing me his own card.

"Maybe you two should exchange cards also," I chuckled. "I'm not sure if I'll be passing this way again, but something tells me you'll be stopping here periodically on the way to delivering your loads. Maybe you should try hitching your rigs together more often. There's more than one way for the rubber to hit the road when truckers need to take a load off."

I watched the two men exchange cards and head off in different directions from the truck stop, then I breathed a sigh of relief when I got in my car and started it up. I could feel my pussy aching from all the unexpected pounding I'd taken in the glory hole cubicle, and right now I just needed to lie down in a soft, warm bed. But not before I'd taken an hour-long shower to wash all the cum and sweat stains off my crusty body. While I pulled out my smartphone and tapped on the maps app to locate the nearest four-star hotel, I shook my head as I leaned against the front of my steering wheel. That was the craziest and dirtiest thing I'd ever done, but it had been absolutely exhilarating.

"For a good time, indeed," I chuckled to myself as I started up the motor and connected my phone to my car's onboard navigation screen...

~

R*eady for more ladyboy chills and thrills? Read the next volume in Shae's T-Girl Adventures: The Ballerina. Buy direct and save at victoriarusherotica.com. Or download from your favorite online bookstore here: retailer links.*

Stretching the limits of a new friendship...

ALSO BY VICTORIA RUSH

Adult Fairytales:

The Enchanted Forest: An Erotic Fairytale

The Land of Giants: An Erotic Fairytale

The Dragon's Lair: An Erotic Fairytale

Witch's Brew: An Erotic Fairytale

The Mage's Spell: An Erotic Fairytale

The Mermaid Lagoon: An Erotic Fairytale

The Coven: An Erotic Fairytale

Rapunzel: An Erotic Fairytale

The Seven Dwarfs: An Erotic Fairytale

The Land of Mutants: An Erotic Fairytale

The Erotic Temple 1: A Sexy Fairytale

The Erotic Temple 2: A Sexy Fairytale

Erotic Fantasy:

Pirate's Bounty: A Time Travel Adventure

Wild West: A Time Travel Adventure

Private Riley: A Time Travel Adventure

Cleopatra's Secret: A Time Travel Adventure

Bounty Hunter 2125: A Time Travel Adventure

Ninja Assassin: A Time Travel Adventure

The 300: A Time Travel Adventure

Arabian Nights: An Erotic Fairytale (coming soon...)

Lesbian Erotica (Completed Series):

The Dinner Party: Lesbian Voyeur Erotica

The Darkroom: Bisexual Voyeur Erotica

Naked Yoga: Lesbian Transgender Erotica

Nude Cruise: Bisexual Voyeur Erotica

Rush Hour: Taboo Public Sex

The Girl Next Door: First Time Lesbian Erotic Romance

Girls' Camp: Lesbian Group Sex

Wet Dream: Ladyboy Fantasy Erotica

The Convent: Taboo Sex with a Nun

Sex Robot: A Dream Sex Machine

The Personal Trainer: Getting Pumped at the Gym

The Dominatrix: BDSM Lesbian Domination

Webcam Chat: Lesbian Online Sex

Paint Me: A Kinky Bodypainting Workshop

The Toy Party: Girls Sharing Sex Toys

The Costume Party: Strapping One On

Swedish Sauna: Lesbian Group Sex

The Therapist: Taboo Lesbian Erotica

Elevator Shaft: Bisexual Threesomes Erotica

Ladyboy: Lesbian Transgender Erotica

Peep Show: Lesbian Voyeur Erotica

The Dare: Public Sex Erotica

Maid Service: Lesbian Threesomes Erotica

The Hitchhiker: First Time Lesbian Erotica

The Housesitter: Spycam Lesbian Erotica

The Spa: Lesbian Group Orgy

Parlor Games: Blindfold Sex Party

The Exchange Student: First Time Lesbian Erotica

The Hostel: Bisexual Group Erotica

The Harem: Lesbian Erotic Romance

The Orient Express: Lesbian Voyeur Erotica

The First Lady: A Forbidden Lesbian Erotic Romance

The Slave: Lesbian BDSM Erotica

The Masseuse: Lesbian Sensuous Erotica

Too Close for Comfort: Lesbian Forbidden Erotica

Naked Twister: A Wild Party Game

Lexi: The Sex App (Lesbian Fantasy Erotica)

Call Girl: Lesbian Bisexual Threesomes Erotica

Circle Jill: Lesbian Masturbation Workshop

The Viewing Room: Masturbation Voyeur Erotica

Spin the Bottle: A Kinky Party Game

The Hair Salon: Lesbian Voyeur Erotica

Tribadism 1: Girls Only Sex Workshop

Tribadism 2: The Art of Scissoring

Tribadism 3: Threeway Hookups

The Kiss: A Game of Oral Sex

Pledge Week: Sorority Sisters

Carny Games 1: A Wild Sex Party

Carny Games 2: A Kinky Sex Party

Carny Games 3: An Erotic Sex Party

Dreamscape: An Artificial Reality Game

Glory Hole: Guess Who's On the Other Side

Joy Ride: A Late Night Erotic Bus Trip

The Blind Girl: An Erotic Romance

The Polynesian Girl: Series Finale

Ladyboy Erotica:

The Auction: A Ladyboy Surprise

Hot Tub Hotel: Shemale Seduction

Strip Club for Couples: Transgender Erotica

Erotica Themed Bundles:

Voyeur: Lesbian Erotica Bundle

Public Affairs: A Lesbian Anthology

Futa Fantasies: The Ladyboy Collection

Threesomes: The Lesbian Collection

Threesomes - Volume 2: The Lesbian Collection

First Time: A Lesbian Anthology

Hedonism: An Erotic Anthology

Switch Hitters: Bisexual Erotica

Taboo Erotica: The Lesbian Series

BDSM: The Lesbian Collection

Party Games: The Erotic Collection

Party Games 2: The Erotic Collection

All Girl 1: Lesbian Erotica Bundle

All Girl 2: Lesbian Erotica Bundle

All Girl 3: Lesbian Erotica Bundle

All Girl 4: Lesbian Erotica Bundle

All Girl 5: Lesbian Erotica Bundle

All Girl 6: Lesbian Erotica Bundle

Voyeur: Volume 2

Erotic Fairytale Bundles:

Clover's Fantasy Adventures: Books 1 - 5

Clover's Fantasy Adventures: Books 6 - 10

Steamy Time Travel Bundles:

Riley's Time Travel Adventures: Books 1 - 5

Lesbian Erotica Bundles:

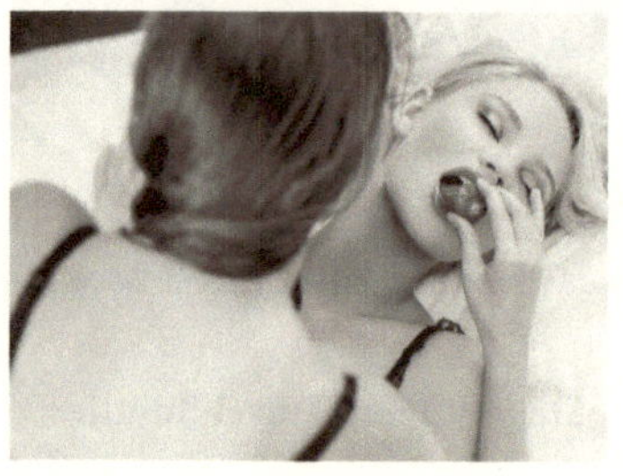

Jade's Erotic Adventures: Books 1 - 5

Jade's Erotic Adventures: Books 6 - 10

Jade's Erotic Adventures: Books 11 - 15

Jade's Erotic Adventures: Books 16 - 20

Jade's Erotic Adventures: Books 21 - 25

Jade's Erotic Adventures: Books 26 - 30

Jade's Erotic Adventures: Books 31 - 35

Jade's Erotic Adventures: Books 36 - 40

Jade's Erotic Adventures: Books 41 - 45

Jade's Erotic Adventures: Books 46 - 50

Jade's Erotic Adventures: Books 51 - 55

Fifty Shades of Jade: Superbundle